Stop Child Abuse

Child Abuse is a sensitive and hard topic to discuss, especially with children. But in today's society, it is occurring more & more every day. This book will help parents & children talk openly and honestly about Child Abuse. Teaching children what Child Abuse is, and how to deal with it. Most important it teaches children what to do to stop the Abuse!

Special Note

It is a proven fact that if children understand all about Child Abuse then they have a much better chance of helping themselves and their friends. We all must step up to the plate and address Child Abuse head on, including its explicit terminology.

This story will teach children what to do if in an abusive situation.

D1258591

Order this book online at www.trafford.com
or email orders@trafford.com

Most Trafford titles are also available at major online book retailers.

Printed in the United States of America.

ISBN: 978-1-4907-1128-7 (sc)
       978-1-4907-1127-0 (e)

Library of Congress Control Number: 2013914254

Our mission is to efficiently provide the world's finest, most comprehensive book publishing service, enabling every author to experience
success. To find out how to publish your book, your way, and have it available worldwide, visit us online at www.trafford.com

Any people depicted in stock imagery provided by Thinkstock are models,
and such images are being used for illustrative purposes only.
Certain stock imagery © Thinkstock.

Trafford rev. 8/30/2013

www.trafford.com
North America & international
toll-free: 1 888 232 4444 (USA & Canada)
fax: 812 355 4082

This book is dedicated to my Dad & Mom,
Herbert D. & Elaine Fuller.
Thank you both for all the love and support you both
gave me and for being there for me through it all.
I'm also dedicating this book to my Best Friend,
Carl Snider (*My Wise Old Worm*).
Thank you for your Patience, your guidance, your
belief in me. Thanks to you, my glass will never be half
empty!

Without the three of you, none of this would be possible.
I love you all!

By Dawn Fuller

I want to give thanks to God for all of his
Forgiveness and Grace!

"Guess what Looper? It's a snow day and there is no school," said Looper's mom. "Cool! Can I go sledding with Woolly Bear and Julia?" asked Looper. "You may," answered Looper's mom. "I am just going to sleep for a little longer, and then I'll get ready," replied Looper.

As Looper, Julia, and Woolly Bear were climbing the hill to go sledding, Julia noticed Rosa building a snowman by herself. She looks so sad, thought Julia. "Looper and Woolly Bear, Do you think Rosa is ok?" asked Julia. "She hasn't been talking," said Looper. "She hasn't been playing with anyone either." added Woolly Bear, "Let's see if she would like to go sledding with us."

"Hey Rosa, do you want to go sledding with us?" asked Looper. "No, not today," sighed Rosa. "Come on Rosa, it'll be fun" said Julia. "Oh, alright," replied Rosa.

On the way down the hill, Julia and Rosa's sled tipped over. "**OUCH!**" cried Rosa, as she grabbed her arm. "Are you ok? That's a big bruise on your arm, did that just happen?" asked Julia. "No, I fell down yesterday and hurt my arm, I just landed on it," replied Rosa.

"You have to be more careful, that's a really big bruise," said Julia. All of sudden Rosa started to cry. "Should we go get help?" asked Woolly Bear. "NO, don't do that, I'll get in trouble if you tell!" yelled Rosa. "Why would you get in trouble? You didn't do anything wrong." said Looper. "If you tell, my dad will be really mad at me." cried Rosa. "Your dad will be mad because you got hurt?" asked Looper. "I don't understand!"

NO, don't do that!

"No, that's not it. Do you guys pinky swear that you won't tell anyone my secret?" asked Rosa. "We pinky swear!" replied Looper, Julia, and Woolly Bear.

Rosa then started to tell them about how her dad abuses her and her twin brother, Rubus. "You need to tell your mom," said Looper. "I tried but she doesn't believe me. I don't know what to do," sobbed Rosa. "You should ask the Wise Old Worm what to do," said Looper, "You can trust him and he always knows what to do." Rosa agreed to ask the Wise Old Worm what she should do.

Looper explained to the Wise Old Worm what was happening with Rosa and Rubus. The Wise Old Worm told Rosa how proud he was of her for telling her friends the truth about her father.

"I know that telling the truth is a very hard, embarrassing, and scary thing to have to do. Telling someone will make it stop. If you do not tell, life will get harder. It can harm the way you think and feel about others and yourself," explained the Wise Old Worm.

The Wise Old Worm then told Rosa how important it is to tell someone who cares about her and who she trusts. "An example of someone to tell would be a Parent, Grandparent, Aunt, Uncle, Friend, Principal, Teacher, School Counselor or a Police Officer."

"Anyone that cares about you will want to help you. If someone doesn't listen or believe you, you need to keep telling, until someone does. Don't ever give up!" Stated the Wise Old Worm.

The next day after school, Rosa stopped to talk to her teacher, Miss Laurel. "There's something that I need to tell you, but it's kind of hard to talk about," said Rosa. "Would you please help me?"

Rosa then explained to Miss Laurel what has been happening to her and her brother, Rubus. Miss Laurel told Rosa how sorry she was and how she knows that it took a lot of courage to tell her. "I am going to help you Rosa. The first thing we have to do is talk to Mr. Chestnut, our Police Officer, and Mrs. Poinsettia, our School Counselor." said Miss Laurel.

"I understand how terrifying it is to tell, but telling about the abuse will help make it stop!" said Mrs. Poinsettia. She then told Rosa that she was going to have to take her and her brother, Rubus, to a safe place for a few days. Mr. Chestnut then explained to Rosa that her father may be taken away from the home and/or arrested.

Mrs. Poinsettia and Mr. Chestnut took Rosa to her house to tell her mother and father that they were going to take Rosa and Rubus to a safe place for a few days. Rosa's dad, Mr. Crocus, was taken away. He was not allowed to be near Rosa and Rubus again, unless he learns to be a better father.

A few days later on Christmas Eve, Rosa and Rubus returned home to their mother. It was the best Christmas the three of them ever had. Rosa knew she had done the right thing and she was happy.

The End

Looper

Stop Child Abuse

Child Abuse is a sensitive and hard topic to discuss, especially with children. In today's society it is occurring more and more every day. This book will help parents and children talk openly and honestly about Child Abuse. Teaching children what Child Abuse is, and how to deal with it. Most important it teaches children what to do to stop the Abuse!

Special Note

It is a proven fact that if children understand all about Child Abuse then they have a much better chance of helping themselves and their friends. We all must step up to the plate and address Child Abuse head on, including its explicit terminology.

4 Types of
Child Abuse
1. Physical
2. Emotioal
3. Sexual
4. Neglect

Abuse
is BAD

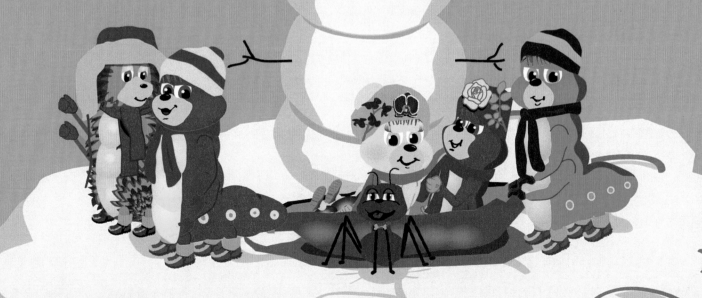

Physical

- **Beating**
- **Slapping**
- **Hitting**
- **Pushing**
- **Shaking**
- **Hair-pulling**
- **Throwing**
- **Pinching**
- **Biting**
- **Choking**
- **Kicking**
- **Burning with cigarettes, scalding water, and/or other hot objects.**

Severe Physical Punishment

Emotional

I HATE YOU! YOU'RE SO STUPID! I CAN'T STAND YOU!

Terrorizing (Scare)
- Yelling and/or threatening a child with extreme punishment
- Abusing another, such as a parent, a sibling, or even a pet
- Playing on childhood fears
- Threatening to leave or get rid of a child
- Smashing things

Corrupting
- Showing a child violence and/or sexual behavior
- Wanting a child to be destructive and/or do bad things

Isolating
- Keeping children away from other children and/or adults

Rejecting
- Being pushed away
- Ignored
- No hugs, Kisses, or other signs of love

Bullying
- Making fun
- Name Calling
- Threatening
- Humiliating
- Belittling
- Shaming
- Teasing

Sexual

- Touching and/or kissing a child's genitals/privates
- Making a child touch and/or kiss an adult's genitals/privates (vagina, breasts, anus, penis, or testicles)

Bad Touches!
Bad Secrets!

Exposing Children to Adult Sexuality
- Performing sexual acts in front of a child
- Exposing genitals
- Telling dirty stories
- Showing pornography to a child

Violations of Bodily Privacy
- Taking pictures of a child with no clothes on
- Forcing a child to undress
- Spying on a child in the bathroom and/or bedroom
- Excessive tickling and/or hugging

Neglect

Physical Neglect

o Not providing a child with food and/or water

o Not providing a child with the proper clothing for the weather

o Not helping and teaching a child with personal hygiene

o Not providing a safe, clean home

o No supervision, child being left alone

Medical Neglect

o Not taking a child to the dentist when needed

o Not taking a child to the doctor when needed

Educational Neglect

o Not sending a child to school

Emotional Neglect

o Not providing a child with love and affection

NO ATTENTION!
NO HUGS!
NO LOVE!
ABANDON!

Feeling Unwanted!

Failing to provide children's basic needs.

The Effects of Child Abuse
Physical Effects

- Extreme hunger
- Dehydration
- Malnutrition
- Minor and/or major bruises or cuts
- Bite marks
- Burns
- Severe broken bones
- Hemorrhage
- Shaken baby syndrome
- Death

- Cardiovascular problems
- Bad dreams
- Sleeping disorders
- Bed wetting
- Learning problems
- Easily startled
- Stuttering
- Scars
- Difficulties in attention and concentration
- Pain and emotional suffering

The physical effects can be temporary. The pain and suffering they cause a child could be life long!

Psychological and Behavioral Effects

- Depression
- Anger
- Emotionally numb
- Anxiety
- Chronic pain
- Panic attacks
- Fear
- Aggressive behavior
- Running away
- Lying
- Stealing
- Shyness
- Violent and/or criminal behavior
- Alcohol and/or drug abuse
- Crave high-risk, stimulating, and/or dangerous experiences
- Risky and/or compulsive sexual behaviors
- Academic difficulties
- Self-injury and/or suicide attempts

- Relationship difficulties
- Inability to trust
- Withdrawal
- Self-blame
- Shame
- No confidence
- Low self-esteem
- Failure to thrive
- Eating disorders
- Dissociative states

Societal Effects

- Violence and/or Crime
- Society as a whole, pay billion's a year due to child abuse

If you or someone you know needs help due to child abuse or neglect, please contact Child Help USA at 1.800.4 A Child (1.800.422.4453)

References

Child Welfare Information Gateway. (2008). Definitions of Child Abuse & Neglect.

Retrieved from https://www.childwelfare.gov/can/defining/-2-4.pdf

Child Welfare Information Gateway. (2008). Long-term Consequences of Child

Abuse and Neglect. Retrieved from

http://www.childwelfare.gov/pubs/factsheets/long_term_consequences.cfm

National Clearinghouse on Child Abuse and Neglect Information. (2005).

Long-Term Consequences of Child Abuse and Neglect. Retrieved from

http:// http://nccanch.acf.hhs.gov -1-4.pdf

Edwards Brothers Malloy
Oxnard, CA USA
October 7, 2013